ONE OF THE DRAGONS

Laura Shenton

ONE OF THE DRAGONS

Laura Shenton

Iridescent Toad Publishing

Iridescent Toad Publishing.

Cover by Blackstone Book Cover Design.

First edition. ISBN: 978-1-913779-65-8

Chapter One

"Clarabellina!"

Clara winced and spun around to face the direction of the voice. She hated her given name. It was almost as unbearable as how much she hated being a dragon shifter. Maybe it had been intended as a portmanteau of Clarabelle and another name ending in 'ina'. Whatever it was, her mother must have been more than a little inebriated when she had picked it out for her.

"What's up?" Clara asked, striding over to Lucian.

Lucian's expression grew solemn as he surveyed her.

"A little bird tells me that you don't plan on joining us at the meeting tonight. Is that right?" he asked. "I suppose you want to spend time with that human instead."

Having noticed the disdain in Lucian's voice as he'd uttered the word 'human', Clara folded her arms defensively.

"Do you have a problem with who I'm seeing?" she demanded.

"It doesn't matter what I think," he retorted. "It's just the way things are. It's not feasible to establish a long-lasting relationship with a human. He will depart this life long before you do, by several decades. What will you do when people start mistaking you for his grandchild? It will never work."

Exasperated, Clara raised her hands to the sky before dropping them to her sides.

"You're joking, right?" she replied. "Darryl and I have only been together for a few months. We haven't even broached the subject of my true nature."

Lucian breathed a deep sigh and ran his hand through his cropped auburn hair. His brow wrinkled as he glowered at Clara.

"Come on, Clara. You know how it is," he said.

"The humans have no regard for us. In fact, you've probably heard tales of them relentlessly pursuing us. Why bother with this particular human? Don't you care about the rest of us?"

Clara snarled, her nostrils flaring as she felt the beginnings of a burning sensation charging along her shoulder blades.

Lucian swiftly stepped back. As he let out another deep sigh, Clara knew that it was futile to get into an argument with him, and so instead, she pivoted and strode away.

She knew that if he really wanted to, he could call her back and demand her attendance at the meeting. She sensed, however, that he wouldn't. Despite his position of head of the dragon shifter alliance, imposing his will on any member wasn't Lucian's way. He was a leader who maintained that everyone had free will, and that they were superior to their more bestial nature.

It was a philosophy that Clara wasn't entirely convinced of. She glanced down at the mottled skin on her hands, dry from where her scales had emerged earlier that day. She was doubtful that she could ever think of herself as a virtuous individual.

She shook her head, and then thrust her hands back into her pockets, acknowledging that she mustn't indulge such a negative train of thought. She needed to get a move on; Darryl was probably waiting for her.

The thought made Clara smile as she walked inside the alliance headquarters, a grand building by any stretch of the imagination, and made her way towards her bedroom.

I wonder what Darryl would do if he knew the truth about me.

Darryl was unapologetically outspoken. He was perfectly matched to his job in the city. A successful businessman, he was twelve years older than Clara and had a wealth of life experience, which only served to make him the best in his field. It was one of the qualities that had endeared Clara to him in the first place. She wished that she could be as bold and outgoing, and not plagued by an overwhelming undercurrent of anxiety that hit her so often.

Clara stormed into her bedroom and forcefully shut the door, turning the lock to ensure privacy. Her ears picked up raised voices echoing in the hall, but she paid them no mind as she quickly retreated to the bathroom to vigorously exfoliate the dead skin that she was so conscious of. After showering, she dressed herself in ripped jeans and a black tank top, a straightforward yet sufficient outfit for her plans with Darryl. The new history museum was the destination for their upcoming outing.

Clara stared at her reflection in the mirror, her hand pulling nervously at the bottom of her top. Doubts nagged at her as a little voice in her head asked if her outfit was good enough for the date. Darryl had never given her any reason to be insecure, but she still wanted to look good for him.

Despite Clara's efforts to keep cool and collected, her mind continued to whirl as she descended the stairs and exited the alliance headquarters. Waiting for her outside, was a modest-but-classy black car. As she approached it, Darryl quickly got out and opened the passenger side door for her, gesturing for her to get in. Still feeling self-conscious, and replaying in her mind the conversation that she'd just had with Lucian, doubts continued to nag at her.

Chapter Two

"Your red-haired friend was looking at me a bit suspiciously," said Darryl. "It's as though he was expecting me to break in."

Clara gritted her teeth in frustration. She still couldn't think of a suitable explanation that she could give to Darryl for the alliance headquarters. Keeping the alliance safe was paramount, but she wasn't willing to lie either. The alliance was her only family, and she couldn't risk endangering them – not after what had happened to another alliance not that long ago. One of the members had made the mistake of showing their real form to a human, who reacted in horror and began hunting all of their associates. In the end, all of those dragon shifters were killed.

"Clara?"

"Oh, right, yes. Sorry," Clara uttered as she looked at Darryl. "I was miles away."

"So I've noticed," said Darryl, smiling gently at her. "I've been trying to get your attention for a good few minutes now. Are you ok?"

Clara sighed and shrugged her shoulders. She nervously played with the jewellery on her right index finger, a single golden ring.

"I've just been a bit distracted recently," she said. "Things have been a bit tense at home."

"What is it?"

"It's nothing, really," she replied. "Anyway, I'm here with you now. I want to focus on that."

Darryl smiled and grabbed Clara's hand, bringing it to his lips and planting a gentle kiss on the back of it.

"Well, whatever it is, you can always talk to me about it," he said in a soothing voice. "I'm not here to judge you – if there's anything you need from me, you only have to ask."

Darryl's kindness made Clara feel guilty that she could only tell him so much.

She shakily nodded, her throat tightening. Lying to Darryl was the last thing she wanted to do, but the risk of revealing her true identity was simply too great. She didn't know why he had chosen to stay with her, and she felt that if he found out who she really was, he would leave her. But telling the truth felt wrong; it could cost not only her life, but that of everyone else in the dragon shifter alliance.

Clara's thoughts raced through her mind as she stared out of the car window at the passing townsfolk. How could she possibly unleash the secret of her inner dragon to Darryl? She had been keeping the truth hidden away for so long; it seemed impossible to find the words and let him in on her dark, dangerous secret. Her life had always felt so divided – she had never fitted in anywhere. With the dragon alliance, she felt no connection, only a sense of security in numbers. With Darryl, she could be herself, but only to an extent. She was beginning to wonder if the alliance's "safety in numbers" mentality was a lie, but it was the lie that kept her alive.

Darryl drove to the side of the road before switching off the car's engine. He turned in his seat to face Clara.

"Come on, Clara. Talk to me," he said. "I know you can be in your own world sometimes, but this is something else. If it's me, you can tell me. Of course I'd be hurt, but I can take it. Please, talk to me."

"It's not you, it's me," Clara said.

She felt her cheeks burn as she attempted to give Darryl's hand a reassuring squeeze. Unconvinced, he pulled it away.

"Then let me in," he said. "I care about you very much, and as wild as I am about you, I'm not a mind-reader."

Clara cringed, ashamed and pissed off with herself. She felt so strongly for Darryl and she hated the fact that she had to be so closed-off to him in some ways.

"There's just a lot going on at home," she said. "And I don't want to put you off."

"That's understandable," said Darryl, his exasperation evident as he worked his fingers through his midnight-black hair. "I just don't want you to shut me out. I'm serious about being with you."

Clara fought to stifle her emotions, but her bottom lip quivered, exposing the fear she was trying to hide.

"I'm sorry," she said. "I'm so damn sorry."

Before Darryl could reply, Clara had already opened the car door and stepped out. She slammed it behind her and then made her way into the woods that bordered the road. She hated the thought of upsetting Darryl, or saying the wrong thing to him. How could he ever accept her if he knew that sometimes, she turned into a dragon? She could already feel herself losing control. A distinctive aching burn was surging through her spine. It was probably for the best that she had left the car; otherwise, Darryl would have seen her true form.

Clara trembled as large scaly wings began to push through and protrude from out of her back. She hurried further and further into the trees, pushing herself as hard as she could until the sound of Darryl's voice became nothing more than a distant whisper. Only then could she relax and let her true form emerge – that of a dragon.

One Of The Dragons

Chapter Three

Morphing into another form was challenging for all dragon shifters. The most difficult aspect was the excruciating sensation of bones cracking and reforming into a different configuration. For some, their human-presenting physique would shrink if their dragon form was smaller. Their organs would rearrange to fit their post-shift body. It was the same for shifters whose dragon form was larger than their human body, but instead, their bones would turn soft before stretching and hardening.

Although it made her shift no less agonising, shrinking or stretching had never been a factor for Clara; in her dragon form, her body was the same size as that of her human one. The severity of the situation around her always determined the extent of her shift; sometimes her whole body and head would turn into that of a dragon, but other times she would maintain her human body and head.

Regardless of the extent of her shift, she always gained large wings and a tail, both of which enabled her to fly. Either way, every time that she morphed into her dragon form, the entirety of her human body would suffer the pain of having to accommodate the shift. The metamorphosis was something that she had always found unpleasant.

Bent low, with some of her human features unchanged, and highly aware of the weight of her wings on her back, Clara quivered in the wet mud, her breaths coming in heavy gasps. On this occasion, her transformation had left her feeling particularly weak. The toll it took on her was always evident. Her struggle with the shift was well known amongst the dragon alliance. Though each of them suffered through the pain of a shift, their recovery time was much shorter. Clara, however, would always feel sick – an indication that something about it didn't feel right.

As Clara gathered her balance on her arched claws, she mused that the whole process was anything but natural. She wriggled her scaled toes, relishing the sensation of the spongy earth beneath them, while her heightened senses took in the sounds of the woods. Even in the distance, Darryl's voice echoed, calling out for her. Clara had mixed feelings about his determination, both admiring and resenting it.

Glancing back in the direction of the car, she contemplated her options. She could always shift back and go over to Darryl, engaging in yet another difficult conversation. Alternatively, she could go to the alliance headquarters. Although she would have to feign camaraderie with the others once there, the choice was a simple one to make.

***

The alliance headquarters was a bustling and lively place. With a multitude of dragon shifters living there, complete silence was impossible. Clara stood inside the small shed located on the alliance's outdoor territory surrounding the house. She proceeded to retrieve her personalised plastic storage container, from which she took out a new set of clothes to wear.

Looking dishevelled – or even being stark naked – in front of other dragon shifters was of no concern. For many, it was an inevitable outcome. During the transformation process, depending on the physique of dragon that each human morphed into, clothes were prone to being ripped, or in some cases, left in complete tatters.

Now in her human form, Clara got dressed quickly and crept into the alliance headquarters through the rear entrance. She was immediately struck by the overwhelming sense of disorder that filled the air. The clamour of raised voices emanating from the meeting chamber on the opposite end of the house was audible to her already.

The volatile situation was hardly a shock; such turbulent occurrences were commonplace within the alliance.

Exhaling a deep sigh, Clara meandered through the desolate corridors en route to the alliance's gathering, hoping to gain insight into what was going on. She hoped, at least, that whatever it was, it would distract Lucian from quizzing her about why she had ditched her date and decided to attend.

The meeting chamber was solely occupied by alliance members over the age of eighteen, conversing animatedly with one another. Clara was relieved by this development, as it implied that she could remain unnoticed by taking a seat in the rearmost corner of the chamber.

No such luck though!

"Clarabellina!" Lucian proclaimed as a grand announcement. "How wonderful of you to grace us with your presence! What brings you here, pray tell? Have you grown weary of your human companion at last?"

Lucian stood atop the table positioned at the chamber's focal point, taking charge of the audience's focus. Clara felt a flush of embarrassment heat up her cheeks, while her eyes welled up with tears as she lowered herself further into her chair. A satisfied grin spread across Lucian's face as he directed a nod towards her. The gesture only served to heighten Clara's disdain, for it was as though he was acknowledging that he was right in his assertion that her relationship with Darryl – or indeed any human – could never work.

Clara heaved a deep sigh and cleared the tears from her face, which had begun to trickle down gradually. Emotionally, she had always needed to be self-reliant. As she sat there at the back of the meeting chamber, she told herself that she would just have to get used to being alone, and that although she hadn't officially broken up with Darryl, the way she had walked out on him mid-conversation had probably sealed the relationship's fate.

"It appears that Clara has concluded her dalliance with a human," Lucian announced proudly, his voice dominating the entire chamber. "Anyway, I've gathered you all here today because there's something urgent to be discussed, namely the cause of the death of some humans nearby."

The alliance members in attendance ceased their chatter, causing Clara to wince in embarrassment and wish she could vanish without a trace. Although she had previously killed a hunter, it had been a matter of self-preservation because the hunter had been poised to kill her. Lucian was aware of this. The alliance had a standing policy that any human who discovered their existence had to be eliminated. The presence of a dragon in the woods would certainly arouse suspicion and indicate that something was out of place.

"According to reports, humans have been disappearing from their beds in the middle of the night," said Lucian. "Initially, the authorities believed that the culprit was someone from outside the area. However, most recently, investigators have started to change their focus and tactics towards the possibility that the culprit could be a local."

As his partner approached, Lucian took a step back. Sarah was an attractive woman, but she had little going on upstairs. Clara sighed and gazed out of the window into the inky darkness of the night. Although Sarah's ties to the local law enforcement could be valuable at times, she was otherwise a shallow and uninteresting person.

"The police have begun their search through the woods, in search of the children who have gone missing," Sarah announced. "Recently, a group of adults have also disappeared. Furthermore, the police have discovered extensive claw marks on a bed frame belonging to a man. He remains unaccounted for, having gone missing just two nights ago."

As Sarah recounted the disturbing events as though they were just some kind of spooky tale, Clara struggled to take her seriously. Agitated, Clara glanced around to see where Lucian had gone, but he was nowhere to be found. She tried to sit up straighter, hoping to hear any sign of his return, but the commotion caused by Sarah made it impossible to hear anything else.

Clara was gazing out of the window when she suddenly caught sight of a pair of headlights shining through the glass. Her stomach fluttered with nervous energy as she recognised the familiar form of Lucian silhouetted in the light. She watched, transfixed, as he strode purposefully towards the car, his broad shoulders tense as he moved.

"Darryl!" Clara exclaimed, too surprised to stop herself from speaking out.

She sprinted past the curious dragon shifters, her agile movements rivalling that of any human.

Despite her speed, she couldn't get there in time. Lucian was already conversing with Darryl by the time she made it outside. Determined, Clara positioned herself between the two, earning an uncomfortable look from Darryl, who already seemed upset.

"Clara?" he said shakily. "I was so worried about you. Are you ok?"

It surprised Clara that Darryl had followed her home. He had never seen anyone else in the alliance before and the situation felt uncomfortable.

Lucian adopted a defensive stance, flexing his

biceps and crossing his arms.

"You're an unexpected visitor," he snapped at Darryl. "Ordinarily, individuals who come by must communicate with me initially. I perceive you as being excessively curious and lacking in justification for being here. Leave the premises at once, or I shall call the police."

Lucian's words caused Darryl's jaw to drop in surprise. Clara was burning with embarrassment.

It was unusual for Lucian to act so aggressively towards strangers, especially given his generally amiable demeanour. Although Clara was aware of his unease around humans, she had never seen him act like this.

"There's no need to speak to him like that," Clara said, surprised by her own words.

"You came home looking so agitated," retorted Lucian, his voice deep and firm. "In fact, I have never seen you in such a state. How dare they! Furthermore, I'll be damned if I'm going to let them, of all things, waltz into our residence."

"It really isn't like that," Clara explained, her tone laced with urgency.

Darryl could be in danger here, and it's all my fault.

Lucian seemed to have no intention of leaving. Clara knew that she needed to stand her ground with him. She sighed and pointed to the house.

"Please," she said to Lucian, her tone calmer than before. "Give us some privacy for a moment. Trust me to deal with this. I know what I'm doing."

Lucian took a few moments to observe Darryl before conceding with a nod. As he sauntered back to the house, he popped his knuckles. Even though he was out of sight, Clara could feel his gaze on her. She was aware that like the other dragon shifters, he would keep an eye on them from the window.

"Darryl," she said solemnly. "I'm so sorry. I didn't mean to cause you so much worry. It's just that the conversation was getting so heavy and I..."

"I'm here because I need to know that you're ok," Darryl interrupted.

"You deserve better," Clara said defiantly. "I'm

loaded with so much baggage."

"That doesn't put me off," Darryl said with confidence.

He walked closer towards Clara and took her hand in his. He looked deep into her eyes.

"You know I'm not a man who would waste my own time," he said firmly. "I am fully invested in this. I am fully invested in *you*."

With that, he leaned in to kiss Clara. She was too enchanted to reject him, and she couldn't deny her feelings. Yet still, in the back of her mind, she couldn't get past the guilt that he didn't deserve to be lied to.

Trying hard to shove the awful dilemma from her train of thought, with her lips locked onto his, and with her arms around his firm body, she knew that she needed him.

One Of The Dragons

Chapter Four

After Clara had planned a date with Darryl for the following evening, he departed. Upon returning to the meeting chamber, she felt herself flush as all eyes were on her.

"What was that all about?" Lucian demanded.

Feeling uncomfortable, Clara remained silent. With the group waiting in anticipation of a response, her face reddened with embarrassment as she retreated to the corner of the chamber.

Lucian climbed back onto the conference table, whilst other members of the alliance distributed files to everyone in attendance. Clara hesitated to open hers, but eventually did so. The contents included a photo of the bed that belonged to the most recent kidnapping victim. There were deeply-etched claw marks on the floor beside it that could have only been left by a monstrous creature. Another photo featured a man who had gone missing. He had dark hair, an angular nose, piercing eyes, and a gentle smile, somewhat resembling Darryl. Clara was motionless as she stared at the image, afraid that Darryl could easily be the next victim.

"It's certain that a dragon shifter is responsible for this heinous act," Lucian announced. "Currently though, we don't have enough information to enable us to identify the perpetrator. There are countless potential suspects to consider."

He gestured towards a screen, which displayed images of criminal dragon shifters known to the alliance.

"Hang on a moment!" Olivia, the woman sitting next to Clara, interjected. "How can we assume that all potential suspects have already been identified? What if it's a dragon shifter unfamiliar to the alliance? Surely it is damaging to assume that whoever is behind this could be known to us?"

"Look," said Lucian, sighing and folding his arms across his muscular chest. "The authorities have provided us with comprehensive descriptions of the rogue shifter."

"But nobody knows if every single suspect has been accounted for!" Olivia retorted. "I just think that by asking everyone here to engage with this, you're not doing the alliance any favours."

Lucian bellowed with anger, prompting small iridescent scales to emerge from beneath the skin on his hands.

Olivia refused to back down. She stealthily stood up and climbed onto the conference table, glaring at Lucian the whole time.

Clara recoiled in her chair, attempting to minimise her presence. Whenever the alliance engaged in heated arguments like this, it usually signalled an impending brawl. It was uncommon, however, for the head of the alliance to participate in such disputes. Everyone knew that to challenge the leader was to agree to a battle to the death.

Olivia was well aware of the rule, having been informed of it upon her arrival at the alliance's perimeter. She had sought refuge from the turmoil of her previous alliance, yet she now found herself opposing the very individual who had offered her shelter and protection.

Clara knew that Olivia was shrewd and wouldn't initiate a confrontation without being prepared to follow it through. She also suspected that there was an ulterior motive behind Olivia's actions – one that could potentially endanger others in the alliance.

Sarah grasped Olivia's arm, her voice hushed and urgent.

"Come on, Olivia," she said. "Sit down. This really isn't worth it."

Olivia brushed Sarah's hand away. She had no intention of having someone watch over her. She was determined to issue a challenge that she could not retract.

The meeting chamber was quiet as the dragon shifters observed the spectacle occurring before them. Lucian maintained his composure as he stared Olivia down, attempting to keep his anger in check. With his muscles coiled, he gave a resolute nod.

"Very well," he said. "It's no secret what you're striving for. State your intent or withdraw your challenge. But I caution you, I will defeat you and you will perish. That peaceful life you sought – the one with a family and a sense of belonging? You can forget about that if you go through with this. Even if you manage to emerge victorious, there will be no welcoming embrace. The alliance will resent you. They'll obey you only because you defeated me, not because they believe you're the right leader."

Clara recoiled in shock as she observed white-hot scales emerging from Olivia's skin. The bones along Olivia's nose then began to rearrange themselves into the shape of a snout with large, flaring nostrils. Despite the pain that came with the beginnings of a shift, Olivia stood her ground, refusing to show any weakness or fear. Clara couldn't help but respect her strength and bravery, even if she was going about things the wrong way.

"The possibility that the alliance may not accept me is not a concern that would stop me from challenging you," Olivia announced boldly to Lucian. "Under your so-called leadership, the alliance is being led astray. I'm sure I'm not the only one here who feels this way. I feel that it is my obligation to speak up."

"Enough talk," Lucian said with a snarl. "Either make your challenge known, or leave the alliance now."

A smirk tugged at Olivia's lips.

"Very well," she said. "I, Olivia Hallson, formally challenge you, Lucian Freeley."

"The gauntlet has been thrown," Lucian declared, acknowledging the challenge. "On Friday night – when the next snow falls – our fates shall be decided."

As Olivia jumped down from the table, whispers and murmurs echoed throughout the chamber.

"Be prepared for your demise," she taunted Lucian, her words following behind her as she sauntered away.

Chapter Five

In the elegant restaurant, Clara and Darryl sat opposite each other. The cosy and intimate atmosphere was perfect for their date. Darryl had ordered the carbonara. He neatly twirled the cream-coated spaghetti around his fork. Tidy and organised, he was so different to Clara and her hectic ways, and yet, somehow, they melded together so well.

"You're watching me," said Darryl, a playful smile on his face.

Clara blushed.

"It's fine by me," he said. "I'm glad to be here with you."

With a gentle touch, he raised his free hand to caress Clara's cheek for a brief moment, causing her blush to turn a deep crimson. Shaking her head, she let her hair tumble down. Just as she had been aiming for, it covered her face like a veil. Swiftly, Darryl brushed it away, gazing at Clara with intense sincerity.

"You're beautiful, Clara," he said. "You don't ever have to be shy around me, although I must say, it's very cute."

Clara struggled to evade Darryl's unwavering gaze, which was becoming increasingly intense. It scared her that she would have to break it off with him should Olivia emerge victorious in the upcoming conflict. With Olivia as leader of the alliance, Clara would never be allowed to see Darryl again. Despite Lucian's frequent disapproval and vocal objections, he was significantly more tolerant of their relationship compared to Olivia, who harboured an intense loathing for humans – even more so than for Lucian's style of leadership.

A sudden pang twisted in Clara's stomach, causing the shy smile to vanish from her face.

"Is everything ok?" Darryl asked.

Clara let out a deep sigh, considering how much she could disclose to Darryl without exposing her true identity. The reality was that no human would be comfortable to learn that their girlfriend was a dragon. Clara had never heard of any human accepting such a revelation. In fact, if their roles were reversed, she was certain that she would find the information difficult to come to terms with. She had never wanted to be a shifter, but somehow, that was the hand that she'd been dealt.

"It's nothing to worry about, really," she finally replied. "I'm just thinking about the weather that's due on Friday. Are you sure you want to go camping in the woods this weekend?"

The voice in the recesses of Clara's mind accused her of lying. The impending danger of Darryl being in the woods on Friday had her worried sick. It wouldn't be safe there. Any human caught in the middle of a dragon battle would stand no chance. In the heat of the moment, there would be no room for rational thinking.

Clara shook her head, her heart heavy with the realisation that she couldn't bear the thought of Darryl going camping that night.

"Don't look so worried," said Darryl. "I've set up my tent in the exact same spot many times before and never had any trouble. It will be nice to be out there in the wild after such a busy week at work."

"Even in the snow?"

"Absolutely!" Darryl enthused. "You know I enjoy the challenge. It would be a missed opportunity not to do it."

Clara's heart pounded with terror. She had hoped that Darryl would cancel the trip, but instead, he would be putting himself not only at the mercy of the freezing temperatures, but at the peril of something dreadful.

"I'm sure it will be all fun and games until a wild animal tries to break into your tent in search of shelter," Clara said.

She had been trying to make a joke of the situation to hide her fear, but there was an element of truth in her words; she didn't want Darryl to come face to face with any wild beast, but least of all, a dragon in full rage.

Darryl simply laughed. His expression then turned to a serious one.

"I wish there was something I could do to help

you with your anxiety," he said sincerely.

Clara couldn't help but be touched by this, even though it wasn't what she was aiming to achieve with the conversation.

"Please, just hear me out," she pleaded. "I'm really concerned about you being out in the woods during the heavy snow. It's just not safe. Can you promise me that you'll stay home on Friday night? I can't bear the thought of something happening to you and you not coming back safely on Sunday."

"Why are you so worried about Friday all of a sudden?" Darryl quipped, an edge of frustration in his tone. "When I last went camping in bad weather, you hardly seemed to give it a second thought."

Clara sighed, her mind racing. She needed to find a convincing way to dissuade Darryl from going to the woods on Friday. It would be so much simpler if she could just be honest with him, but the truth would put them both in harm's way.

It's a cheap shot, but perhaps it's my best bet...

"Ok," said Clara, a sudden playfulness in her

voice. "I think I know how to keep you warm over the weekend. Promise you'll stay home Friday night, and you'll be getting a special visit from me Saturday morning. I want to be handcuffed to your bed."

Darryl's face lit up at this.

"You're a determined little minx, aren't you?" he said, smirking at her as he finished the rest of his meal. "Ok. You've got yourself a deal."

Clara felt an intense wave of relief wash over her. She hated that she had to lie to Darryl, but all the same, at least he would be safe at home.

Chapter Six

On the night the alliance members were due to meet in the depths of the woods, just as the forecast had promised, it was snowing heavily. The group was sure that no humans would be able to find them in such terrible weather. One of the benefits of being a dragon shifter was having some immunity to the cold. Their inner warmth protected them from the bitter chill in the air. Still though, Clara put on a black cardigan and some boots; she wanted to keep dry, and to have sure footing.

Preparing herself for the worst, she quietly stepped out of her bedroom and slowly descended the stairs. Upon approaching the door of the meeting chamber, she found that it was slightly open. She peered inside and saw Lucian in a chair, his hands held firmly together in his lap. Sarah was on one knee, tears streaming down her face with her hands on Lucian's. Both of them were weeping.

Clara stepped away, imagining what it would be like to have someone care for her so deeply; to have a special someone by her side as she stood on the brink of death. More than anything, she wanted Darryl to be that person. But she knew that was impossible; he'd probably be gone long before she was facing death.

Trying to push away her apprehensions, Clara went outside to where the other dragon shifters were already waiting. As a group, they would go into the clearing, but at least one of them wouldn't survive to make it back. Clara had never approved of this way of life within the alliance.

Her presence evoked a sneer from Olivia.

"As soon as I'm the leader, you can say goodbye to that disgusting *human*," she said spitefully.

With her stomach in knots, Clara bowed her head. She was well aware that Olivia wasn't suggesting just a break-up; if given half the chance, she would wickedly rip Darryl to shreds. Scaly dark patches started to appear on Clara's arms, but she knew that it was futile to engage with Olivia. Olivia was a better fighter, and if anyone could defeat Lucian in a battle, it would be her. The other members of the alliance were also convinced of this fact, their eyes streaming with tears as they watched Lucian and Sarah step sorrowfully out of the alliance headquarters.

Carrying a dummy in her mouth, their daughter trailed behind them. No child was exempt from bearing witness to a challenge. Young dragon shifters grew up aware of what it was to be in the alliance.

Clara glanced at Lucian. Although they didn't always see eye to eye with each other, he had always looked out for her. He gave her a subtle nod of acknowledgement. Sarah crouched down to scoop up their daughter.

Solemnly, Clara marched with the alliance down the worn path that had been traversed by others before them. The journey stopped at the sacred fighting grounds, a place where the leader of an alliance and any of their challengers were on equal footing. Having to sit on the sidelines and observe the outcome, no one was allowed to interfere with a duel.

The group ventured into the open area as the snowstorm worsened. Icy flecks of snow danced around them in a blizzard. As the sharp wind blew against her, several tiny-but-vicious hailstones stung Clara's cheek.

Lucian and Olivia stood at the centre of the clearing as everyone else huddled around the edges. The children held tightly onto their parents, petrified for what was about to happen, for they were all about to witness something that would change them forever.

Olivia snorted aggressively before shifting into a large white fire dragon. She quickly took flight, hovering in the sky above the clearing, ready to strike when the moment came. Standing in the snow and looking up as his opponent soared, Lucian morphed into a powerful and agile ice dragon. Clara crossed her fingers behind her back, silently hoping for him to be victorious.

Suddenly, Olivia abruptly changed direction, swooping towards Lucian with her wings spread open. Just short of crashing into him, she breathed a relentless jet of fire at him. He recoiled and snarled in response, and then, in a split second, he was airborne. Hovering just above Olivia's head, he swiped at her with his freezing front claws, forcing her onto the ground. Quickly regaining her footing, Olivia jumped back into the sky.

"I can't bear to watch," Sarah said as she moved to stand closer to Clara.

Clara nodded in agreement. She didn't particularly want to stand with Sarah. The woman was on the brink of losing her partner. All the same though, she wasn't going to cast her aside, not in such dire circumstances.

Lucian grabbed Olivia and violently threw her to the ground, causing the snow beneath her to redden with her blood.

"We really need to talk about you and your human," said Sarah, her voice full of sympathy. "If Olivia kills Lucian, you need to get to Darryl before she can. The two of you should escape together if it comes to that. I will do all I can to delay Olivia for as long as possible."

Clara was stunned. She had always assumed that Sarah was too self-centred to be paying attention to what was going on with her.

"I don't expect you to do that for me," Clara said after a pause.

"Look," said Sarah, sighing and keen to level with Clara. "I don't think you even know why Lucian gives you such a hard time over this."

Lucian let out a livid roar as Olivia's claws scraped across his back. She had already taken off before he could turn around. He quickly flapped his vast blue wings and soared higher than Olivia. She didn't see him until it was too late. Grabbing her with his tail and tightly wrapping his wings around her, he dragged her to the ground. In a fit of fury she managed to break free again.

"I guess he just hates that I'm involved with a human," Clara said.

"It's not like that," Sarah replied. "He's trying to protect you from a difficult situation. You will outlive the human by a long time. So, if Lucian is to accept him into the alliance, he needs to believe that he's worth it. Do you truly think that he is?"

Clara avoided Sarah's gaze. She had only been dating Darryl for a few months, and had yet to reveal her true nature to him. She wasn't sure if she would ever be ready to. With that in mind, she couldn't bring herself to answer Sarah's question.

Clara's daydreaming was interrupted when, out of the corner of her eye, she spotted a human moving around in the trees. Her heart skipped a beat. Someone who had no business being there was standing in the clearing. She was tempted to yell out a warning to run, but that would only put them in danger. She shuddered as she silently prayed that the stranger would notice her first, so that she could signal a warning to them.

All of a sudden, she could hear the human humming to himself. The tune sounded all too familiar.

"Darryl!" she exclaimed.

"Yes, that's who I mean," said Sarah, bewildered by Clara's sudden excitement.

Clara frantically tugged on Sarah's arm and nodded in the direction of where Darryl was stood.

"Look," she hissed in panic. "Darryl is over there. He's surrounded by dragon shifters who are primed to attack."

"You need to get him out of there immediately," Sarah insisted.

In an instant, the focus of the battle shifted. Clara's stomach flipped violently as Olivia roared with determination and flew at full speed towards Darryl.

Clara yelled out in shock, and, without any hesitation, launched herself forwards. She could hear the sound of her clothes tearing as her body rapidly underwent a full transformation. Some of the other shifters followed suit, their need to keep the battle at hand a secret. Clara was certain that some of the less experienced among them wouldn't think twice about moving in for the kill.

Angry and determined, she flew towards Darryl in her dragon form. The transformation from human to dragon had been so fast that she hadn't even registered the pain of it. Using her tail to bat away those who weren't welcome, she shoved her way through the crowd and made it to Darryl's side, determined to protect him.

In absolute shock, Darryl stood there dumbfounded, trembling and not sure what to do. Clara was aware that he was viewing a scene of unspeakable terror; people were turning into dragons before his very eyes! There was no time to be concerned with that though. She needed to take care of Olivia, who was determined to destroy a human.

Clara roared defensively and started to back away from Olivia, forcing Darryl to move back with her. As he screamed out in primitive terror, Clara could only hope that he wouldn't run away from her protection. Olivia was capable of moving much faster than Clara, and there were other shifters now encircling them.

Olivia flapped her wings for more height, and then charged down through the air towards her prey. Clara quickly used her tail to nudge Darryl to the side, causing him to stumble and fall over. In her dragon form, she outweighed him significantly.

With little that she could do to get away from Olivia, Clara knew that she had no choice but to kill her.

With a deep growl, Clara soared into the sky, flapping her rich purple wings. Although not the most skilled fighter, she possessed remarkable accuracy in catching her prey. Upon landing, she seized Olivia in a lethal hold. Despite the fire dragon's attempts to break free, Clara's grasp was too tight. She then summoned all of her dragon power from deep within, ending Olivia with lethal jolts of electricity.

As vibrant veins of golden lightning crackled around Clara's silhouette, the onlookers could only stand in stunned silence. Having transformed from a dragon into a human, Olivia's naked corpse lay limp and motionless in the bloodied snow. With a determined swipe of her claw, Clara pushed the lifeless body to the side.

As another dragon shifter began hurtling towards her, she snarled fiercely. Intercepting the opponent mid-air, she tore mercilessly into their back with her razor-sharp claws. Her body still alight, she incapacitated the foe with jolts of electricity, determined to safeguard Darryl from harm at any cost. She could only wish that he hadn't been so stubborn and had stayed out of the woods.

She looked around defensively to see who else wanted to take her on. She soon noticed that Lucian was standing next to her.

"Sarah and I will take care of the situation here," he said, still exhausted from his own fight with Olivia. "You need to get out of here and take Darryl to safety."

Despite Clara's unhurried approach towards Darryl, he remained visibly distressed. His hysterical whimpering was upsetting to witness. She had never intended for him to discover the truth about her in such a traumatic way.

She meticulously etched a message into the snow with one of her claws.

Climb up on my back.

She stayed crouched down, hoping that Darryl would be able to reach up and pull himself on. Looking around in panic though, he was too scared to do anything.

Empathetic to his situation, Clara sighed in exhaustion, moved forward a little, and proceeded to write a new message.

It's Clara. Come with me, or die here.

Seeing Darryl in such a desolate state made Clara feel helpless. With him still refusing to climb on her back, she cast a swift glance over her shoulder. Some of the less experienced dragons were still fiercely engaged in combat. Having forgotten that there was no longer a need to fight, they charged through the air at each other.

Clara reluctantly decided that with her options running out, she would have to go with one that would inevitably cause her immense pain and deplete her energy reserves.

Closing her eyes and clenching her teeth, she was overcome by excruciating agony, which quickly consumed her body. As her blood boiled and her muscles screamed in pain, every bone in her back fractured and then mended itself. When the tortuous transformation had finally concluded, she was left prostrate on the ground, devoid of clothing, and panting heavily from the ordeal. She peered upwards to see Darryl, who had been stunned into silence, his mouth agape as if on the brink of screaming again.

"I'm going to shift back into my dragon form," she said firmly, looking Darryl straight in the eyes. "You must then mount my back and cling on tight. Is that clear?"

As she began to shift back into a dragon, there was no time for Darryl to answer.

Her breathing laboured, she glared at Darryl, who tentatively approached and then climbed up onto her back. Accepting that it was their final chance to escape the chaos, she tried her best to endure the sting of his tight grip on her weathered scales.

She soared up as high as she could and flew over the woods, back to the alliance headquarters. She didn't allow herself to land until she could see the shed. Darryl then disembarked. He gasped incredulously at her transformation from dragon to human.

"I don't know what to say," he said. "I thought you'd been keeping something from me. But *this*?!"

"I'm sorry," Clara replied.

She moved her hands to cover her naked body, more self-conscious of it than when around fellow dragon shifters.

"Let me get dressed," she said.

As she entered the shed, she discovered that her plastic container was empty. Letting out a disappointed sigh, she stretched up to the highest shelf and retrieved a towel with which to clean herself. After a brisk rubdown, she chucked it into the laundry hamper stationed in the corner. Scouring the shelves, she located Olivia's box. Taking an outfit from it, she quickly got dressed and left the shed to notice that Darryl was sitting huddled up against a tree.

"You're in shock," she said, also shaken. "I think you should go home before the rest of the alliance gets back. Things could get hectic upon their return."

"I don't know who you are," Darryl said as he staggered away, his voice wavering. "I don't know what to believe."

Clara walked into the alliance headquarters. Once inside, she watched from the window as Darryl ambled away. As soon as he had disappeared out of view, she burst into tears.

Chapter Seven

A few weeks later, Lucian addressed everyone in the meeting chamber.

"The individual or group responsible for the assaults on the human population is becoming more ruthless in their approach," he said.

With her gaze fixated on her shoes, Clara felt too numb to engage. A significant part of her soul had been ripped away, and now she saw no value in life. Since the day Darryl had left her standing at the shed following the battle in the woods, she had secretly been following him from afar. It was uncertain as to whether he had disclosed the alliance's existence to anyone, but even if he had, she was past caring. She had told herself that Darryl would be better off on his own, or with another human, and that she just had to accept that. Now that he knew she was a vicious creature, a monstrosity that ended lives, there was no chance of redemption.

Seated beside her, Sarah gave Clara a gentle nudge, urging her to pay attention. Clara couldn't comprehend why Sarah had taken it upon herself to take an interest in her predicament, but nevertheless, she was grateful for the support. After all, ever since Clara had slain one of their own to protect a human, there were members of the alliance who refused to acknowledge her existence. They saw her actions as a despicable betrayal beyond forgiveness.

"The police have reported that a wild creature has been spotted wandering the town at night," Lucian said. "Although they are speculating that it might be a typical wild animal from the woods, I have taken a closer look, and the signs point towards a dragon shifter. What's worse is that this particular shifter seems to be a loner with no regard for the safety of the rest of us. It's therefore imperative that we stay vigilant."

As Sarah nodded in agreement with Lucian, Clara's thoughts drifted away. She gazed out of the window, reminiscing about the good times she had enjoyed with Darryl. Despite knowing it was undeserved, a part of her yearned to see his car pull up outside once more. She couldn't grasp the fact that what she'd had with him was now a thing of the past. Her heart refused to accept that it was over. She wished that she could fix everything that had gone wrong between them, even though she wasn't sure that he'd want to listen to her after what she had done.

"A week from now, we shall embark on a mission to hunt this rogue shifter down," Lucian declared, striding back and forth with his hands clasped behind his back. "When we find them, we will not hesitate to bring them to justice. Due to our recent losses, mandatory training will be enforced for every shifter over eighteen years of age. I expect you all to meet me in the backyard every evening after sunset, where we will train until dawn. It will be our responsibility to keep the town safe through the night, taking turns on patrols."

Clara was filled with dread at the thought of the rogue shifter finding Darryl. Her eyes welled up with tears as she contemplated the grave danger that he could be in. She knew all too well that her own scent still lingered on his car and in his home – a direct consequence of her presence there. It was plausible to assume that the reckless shifter could pick up her scent and trace it back to Darryl.

With a sudden jolt, Clara rose to her feet,

causing her chair to topple over and crash to the ground. She strode across the chamber with purpose and stood before the map, her eyes scanning the pattern of the dragon shifter's attacks. Each new victim brought the shifter closer to the heart of town, its movements spiralling inward with each passing day. The police had identified the pattern, but were clueless about the shifter's true motive. Although the criminal shifter had not yet discovered the alliance or the headquarters, it had picked up on Clara's scent, which was scattered all over town like breadcrumbs.

Clara traced her finger along the twists and turns of the pattern on the map, her mind racing as she tried to pinpoint the shifter's next move. The spiral appeared to be gradually tightening, like a noose around the town. She couldn't shake the feeling of impending doom. With each passing day, the shifter seemed to be drawing closer towards its ultimate goal. Clara knew they had to act fast before it was too late.

"Darryl's apartment!" she blurted out.

Her sudden outburst caused everyone to stare at her.

"What's wrong?" Lucian asked.

Trying to compose herself, Clara took a deep breath. Her face still burned with embarrassment from the attention she'd drawn to herself, but nevertheless, she pointed an unsteady finger at the map and once again traced a line along the spiral towards its centre.

"Mark my words," she said with conviction, her voice laced with a tinge of fear. "The shifter is tracking my scent. It's no coincidence that the attacks are happening in the very same spots where Darryl and I have spent time together. This spiral on the map is tightening, and if it continues this way, the shifter will end up at Darryl's apartment. I'm certain of it."

Lucian strode over to the map and leaned in to inspect it. After a moment, he nodded his head in agreement with Clara's theory.

"It's best to assume that Darryl is a target," he said. "We need to get him to safety, and prepare for the worst. Also, it's likely that the enemy dragon shifter is on the hunt for other dragon shifters in the area – not just Clara."

Someone from the back of the chamber spoke up. It was Hannah, who was cradling her baby in her arms.

"What makes Clara's scent so special that the rogue dragon shifter would follow it?" she asked. "All of us have been around town recently, so why would it be Clara's scent in particular that it's after?"

Lucian pondered over Hannah's question whilst Clara slumped into an unoccupied seat. Gazing down at her quivering fingers, she tried desperately to calm herself down. Her thoughts were consumed by the fact that, thanks to her, Darryl could be in grave danger.

Sarah stood up, and with determined strides, walked over to stand beside Lucian.

"We have all visited the town, but Clara has been spending the most time there, particularly since she started seeing Darryl," she asserted. "Therefore, it's not surprising that her scent would be the most prominent to another dragon shifter."

As the crushing weight of guilt bore down on her, Clara raised her still-trembling hands to her face. She held herself accountable for the peril that now threatened not only Darryl, but the alliance. The mere fact of her existence seemed to have ignited the chaos. If only she had never been brought into this world, if only she had never undergone the transformation into a shifter, perhaps none of this would be happening. But the truth remained that her very presence had attracted the rogue dragon shifter, and that she was to blame for every kidnapping and murder that had taken place.

Lucian spoke up, his voice urgent.

"We need someone to go and get Darryl, but it can't be Clara. If we're correct in our assumption, the shifter could easily track her scent – in combination with Darryl's – back to our headquarters. We can't risk putting everyone in danger like that."

Clara cautiously lifted her head to see who had gently put their hand on her knee. It was Sarah, who was crouching down in front of her.

"Everything will be alright," Sarah said in a reassuring tone. "We will find a solution to this. I will get Darryl myself and bring him back here, alright?"

"Nothing can be done," Clara choked out, tears streaming down her face. "Everyone's life is on the line, and it's all my fault."

"Dragon shifters are always in danger," Sarah

said with empathy. "You never intended for any of this to happen. Don't blame yourself. We will get through this together."

"Darryl won't want me anywhere near him," Clara said, her voice quivering with emotion. "He despises me now."

"I don't think that's the case," said Sarah, putting a comforting hand on Clara's arm. "I've seen the way he looks at you."

"You don't understand," said Clara, pulling away and shaking her head fiercely. "I'm the reason he's in danger. I can't bear to face him. I've always feared that his association with me would put him in harm's way, and now, it has."

Chapter Eight

Just shy of midnight, Sarah drove off in her small blue car. Clara stayed at the window, eyes glued to the vehicle until it disappeared. Less than an hour later, Sarah returned, Darryl beside her in the passenger seat. Clara couldn't tell if he was awake or not. It was entirely possible that Sarah had done something other than simply asking him to get into the car.

Clara made her way downstairs and stationed herself by the building's entrance. Not long after, Sarah appeared with Darryl in her arms, asleep from a sedative. Seeing him like that, Clara couldn't help but feel immense remorse.

She stepped out to Sarah's car and grabbed Darryl's suitcase. She then followed as Sarah carried him upstairs and placed him in the bedroom beside Clara's. Clara's lips twitched into a frown, but she uttered no words as she left the bags in Darryl's new room.

Attempting to get away from Sarah and her endless questions was always a challenge. As soon as Clara had plopped down on her bed, Sarah came into the room, standing there expectantly. Clara remained silent, adamant that with regards to Darryl, there was nothing else to be said.

Sarah let out a sigh and took a seat at the edge of Clara's bed. Clara, feeling reluctant about the impending conversation, groaned and turned onto her stomach in an attempt to ignore it.

"You were just a child when Lucian and I took you under our wing," Sarah said. "I can still vividly recall the image of a lost, injured, weeping little girl who arrived at our doorstep seeking refuge. Back then you were still a mere human. We have never been able to ascertain how you managed to find us. Perhaps it was fate. I am sure you have not forgotten."

"I don't know how I found my way there," Clara confirmed. "I must have been in shock. That particular night is etched in my memory as the most excruciating experience of my life."

"Considering that you were only ten years old at the time, the information you provided about your parents being drug addicts and you living on the streets was the most we could gather," said Sarah. "At times, I find myself pondering about the path your life would have taken if Lucian had not intervened and transformed you."

Clara sighed and shifted her position to face Sarah.

"I've been plagued with the same question for the last thirteen years," she said, her voice tinged with sadness. "Perhaps I would have turned out like my mother. All things considered, maybe that would have been better for me. I resent that in being a dragon shifter, I have no choice in who I can love."

"Lucian still hasn't come to terms with his guilt over that incident," Sarah said candidly. "It appears that you haven't either. For what it's worth though, I'm confident that you will find love. If you wanted to, you could always convert a human into a dragon shifter. You would just need to be sure that you're truly right for each other; there would be no going back."

"And don't I know it!" Clara exclaimed in frustration. "Why would I want to inflict this lifestyle on someone else? Why in the world would I wish to turn someone into a creature like myself? A creature that must fight to live, and potentially kill others to survive?"

"You know it's not as straightforward as that, Clara," Sarah protested. "You yearn for a partner to share your life with, but you may not find that within the alliance. Whether or not you embrace it, you are one of us. When he made the decision to turn you, Lucian did what he believed was necessary to guarantee your survival."

Clara's eyes welled up with tears as she shook her head and turned over on her stomach. She buried her face in the pillow and began to sob. She hadn't asked for this existence. The mere thought of transforming Darryl into a dragon shifter filled her with dread. As much as she yearned to be with him, she couldn't fathom burdening someone she loved with this way of life.

"I have learned from my own experiences that one must make the best of what they have, irrespective of the situation," said Sarah.

The bed moved slightly as she rose to her feet. Clara heard the sound of the bedroom door opening, followed by the sound of footsteps in the hallway.

Once Sarah had closed the door, Clara found herself alone with her thoughts. She turned over onto her back and gazed up at the ceiling. With Darryl now being kept in the alliance headquarters, and in the room next to hers, she knew it would be impossible to avoid him. Accepting that the alliance was keeping him for his own safety, she decided that she needed to put her guilt and shame to one side.

After everything that's happened, the least I can do is be there for him.

She sighed and walked out into the hallway. At the entrance of the room which was now occupied by Darryl, her keen sense of hearing detected the sound of breathing. It wasn't deep enough to indicate that Darryl was asleep. It was most likely that he was wide awake and frightened.

Preparing herself mentally, Clara shakily touched the door handle.

"Are you sure it's a good idea to go in there at the moment?"

Her heart pounding, Clara withdrew her hand from the door and turned around quickly. She immediately found herself facing Lucian, his expression kind rather than domineering. After considering his words, she realised that he was right. She was far too worked-up and tense.

"You look as though you could use some rest," he said gently. "Before you see Darryl, take a moment for yourself first. He needs to see a friendly face soon, but don't go rushing in while you're still on edge. Remember, he was taken from his home in the middle of the night, and is completely in the dark about what's happening."

Clara silently agreed with Lucian's suggestion and retreated to her room. She took a quick shower and changed into comfortable clothing, leaving her damp hair to fall in loose curls around her back and shoulders. As she took a deep breath to steady herself, she came to the conclusion that she would need to speak to Darryl – not just to clear the air, but to prevent any further misunderstandings.

As she cautiously opened the door to Darryl's room, she winced in anticipation. Straight away, his eyes locked onto hers. As his gaze scanned her body up and down, she felt self-conscious as she entered the room.

"What's going on?" he demanded, his voice

shaking with each word. "What do you want from me?"

Taking a deep breath and lowering herself onto the armchair, Clara leaned forward to meet Darryl's gaze.

"I know it's hard to believe," she said. "But when I was a kid, something terrible happened. When I stumbled upon this place in search of help, I was turned for my own protection."

Darryl stared at Clara for a long moment before nodding slowly.

"Ok," he said softly, cocking his head in confusion. "Go on."

"I understand that it's a lot to process. I haven't been honest with you about my true identity, and I am sorry for that. But it wasn't always like this," Clara explained. "When I was young, my parents and I were homeless, living on the streets. One night, we were attacked."

She paused and surveyed the room around her. It had been years since she'd opened up to anyone about what had happened. Not even Lucian and Sarah were privy to every single detail. Although Clara had disclosed most of it to them, some details were just too painful to revisit.

"I only realised that I was covered in my parents' blood after the attack," she continued. "It happened so quickly. I'm still not sure who or what got to them, but I had to run away as soon as I knew I was in danger. My parents were already pretty out of it, and I couldn't save them. I failed them, and that's something that will haunt me forever."

Darryl rose from the bed and approached Clara, who was in tears. Keen to offer comfort, he hugged her tightly. He even leaned in and placed a gentle kiss on her forehead.

"You were just a child, Clara. It wasn't your fault," he whispered. "There was nothing you could have done to save them."

"I... I just feel so guilty," Clara whispered, her voice breaking.

"You don't have to share everything with me at the moment," Darryl said soothingly.

"I want to tell you everything," she said. "I want you to feel that you can ask me anything. I'm so sorry that I didn't tell you before. I didn't want to push you away."

Darryl grunted softly in vague agreement as he continued to hold Clara tightly. As they embraced each other, she let out a soft moan, squirming beneath him. It had been a while since they had last held each other, and both of them had missed it.

"Let's go to bed," he said, taking charge.

"Ok, but we need to talk later," said Clara. "For now though, I'm just glad that you're here with me."

Chapter Nine

Darryl tenderly embraced Clara's nude form as the morning sun began to rise. When daylight shone through the curtains, Clara broke away and sat upright, clutching the duvet to her chest. As she glanced at Darryl, her heart swelled with emotion. She then got out of bed and took a seat in the armchair.

"Hey, where are you off to?" Darryl called out groggily, his voice rough with slumber. "Come back to bed."

"No," said Clara, determined not to give in to the temptation. "The sex was awesome, but we need to talk about why you're here, and what we're going to do next."

"Ok," Darryl uttered as he rose from the bed and began to get dressed. "If you want to talk, let's start with the others here, who are certainly not your family. I'm only here because they abducted me."

After averting her gaze from Darryl, Clara scanned the floor for her own clothes. She got dressed and returned to the armchair. Twirling the ring on her finger whilst looking up at him, the onset of tears stung her eyes. She rallied the last of her courage, determined not to break down in front of him.

"Somewhere out there, an enemy dragon shifter is on our scent, and that's why you were brought here."

"What?! *Our* scent?!" Darryl exclaimed. "You're joking, right? I was abducted because of you?!"

Frustrated, he shook his head in disbelief.

"I suppose you could put it that way," Clara answered. "I did say that we needed to talk about it."

"This is bizarre," said Darryl. "You know I pride myself on being able to cope with all kinds of things. But this?!"

"Things would have been fine if you had only stayed away from the woods that night," said Clara. "You wouldn't have witnessed this side of me, and you wouldn't have been in danger. But no, you ignored my advice because you assumed you knew best. I practically *begged* you to stay out of the woods."

"Oh?! So you didn't plan on letting me know that you occasionally transform into a dragon?!"

Clara rose to her feet and strode across the room, exasperated with the ongoing charade. She understood that Darryl was upset. He had every right to be. She sighed, resigned to the fact that she needed to be clear with him.

"Darryl, you need to listen to me," she said, looking him straight in the eyes. "What I'm going to say might be crucial to your survival. You need to take it seriously, and never forget it. I made a mistake, and I did it because I care about you. Deep down, I've always feared that because of what I am, we'll never be able to have a future together. I thought it would be kinder to keep the truth from you. *You've* done nothing wrong. It's all my fault."

"You fear that we could never have a future together?" Darryl asked. "Is that what you want?"

Clara could feel a blush rising in her cheeks. In wanting to protect Darryl first and foremost, she hadn't intended on revealing the extent of her feelings to him. It certainly added an extra layer of complication to the situation. As a dragon shifter, she knew she was putting both of their lives in danger, and she needed to focus on that. Now though, Darryl seemed more interested in their potential relationship, which only served to overwhelm her all the more.

She sat down on the edge of the bed and finally spoke up.

"My lies have caused you nothing but hurt and confusion, and now, to top it all off, you're in danger, which is why you had to be brought here in the first place. Surely, no matter how much I like you, don't you feel that you deserve better?"

Darryl retreated from Clara and buried himself further into the bed's cushions.

"I'm glad you've told me about how you feel," he said. "I've always told you that you can tell me anything. Of course I'm in shock that you can morph into a dragon. It is evidently a big part of your life. Still though, I don't want to frighten you, but what if there could be an 'us'? Then what?"

"I had thought that an 'us' was off the table," Clara replied. "There's a lot you don't know about dragon shifters. Darryl, I've killed before. What if I lose control and hurt you too?"

Darryl's hand settled gently on Clara's shoulder.

"What if I hurt you?" he asked in a hushed tone. "I know it's overwhelming, and we haven't even been together that long. We haven't even talked for the last few weeks. But you and I have something special. I can feel it, and I've been hoping that you feel it too."

Clara exhaled deeply and pushed Darryl's hand away from her shoulder. She turned her body to face him, and observed intently. His determination was unyielding. A man who refused to be exploited by anyone, he had a strong exterior and would not tolerate any nonsense, yet he was compassionate and affectionate. She couldn't help but think that he was too good for her.

"If we suppose, just for a moment, that you could overlook the fact that I'm a dragon shifter – or maybe even embrace it – what comes next?" she asked.

Avoiding Clara's gaze, Darryl raked his fingers

through his bedraggled hair. He looked as though he was about to cry. Clara couldn't bear the thought of having to break up with him, but she also believed that he deserved to be happy; to have a fulfilling life, and to age gracefully with a human partner who was not a carnal beast.

"I want to know everything – every single detail," Darryl said with determination. "I feel like you and I have something special, something that could be really good. I'm not sure what it is yet, but I know I love who you are."

Clara's heart fluttered. Despite it seeming impossible, Darryl had said he loved her. The conflicting emotions made her want to push away the glimmer of hope. She wanted him to be truly happy and knew that it would be selfish to string him along.

As she gazed at him, she was struck again by his endearing demeanour. She couldn't deny that she was deeply in love with him. His resilience, intelligence, and open-mindedness were all attractive qualities. She realised that if there was any hope for them as a couple, she needed to be completely honest; she needed to give him all of the facts, and then leave the decision of what to do next entirely up to him. No more hiding. No more deceit.

"I want to know everything," Darryl said again. "All the details about our future together, if that's a possibility."

After contemplating for a few moments, Clara determined that it would be most effective to explain what the ultimate outcome would be.

"The truth is that I will outlive you by a significant number of years," she said. "At least fifty, but probably closer to a hundred. There will come a point where people assume that you're my parent, and then eventually, my grandparent. Our relationship dynamic will change."

"We've already got a bit of an age gap," Darryl said, half jokingly.

"I'm serious," Clara insisted. "I need you to really think about this."

Darryl had probably been trying to lighten the mood a little, but his body language told a different story. He fiddled with a thread dangling from his shirt as he tried to digest the information. Clara had moved from the bed to the floor, and was now leaning against the armchair. She found it more comfortable to discuss their future with a bit of space between them. She was starting to wonder whether it might have been simpler to convey everything in writing. That way, she could have avoided seeing the strain on Darryl's face as he struggled to grasp the magnitude of the situation.

"So when I am unable to take care of myself, you would have to be my caretaker?" he finally said. "I couldn't ask you to do that, Clara."

"Even if you decided to end our romantic relationship, I would still be there to take care of you," said Clara. "I'll always want to know that you're ok, regardless of what happens between us."

"You make it sound like you plan on stalking me," he quipped.

He chuckled softly, this time succeeding to break the sombre atmosphere of the conversation.

Despite her sadness, Clara managed a smile. Her feelings for Darryl were genuine, and she truly wanted to take care of him. However, the thought of the alliance intervening if he ever revealed their secret made her uneasy. They were always watching, ready to step in if necessary, and the consequences would not be pleasant. The mere thought sent a chill down Clara's spine.

Darryl furrowed his eyebrows and moved towards the end of the bed, positioning himself onto his front.

"What's the matter?" he asked, observing Clara's ghostly expression.

"If you were to tell anybody about the alliance, they would have to kill you," she stated bluntly.

Darryl's face turned pale and his hands trembled as he clung to the quilt on the bed and grabbed a pillow. After a moment, he nodded slowly and took a deep breath.

"I understand," he said, his voice low. "It's brutal, but I think I understand."

"If you were to tell an outsider about the alliance, it's unlikely that anyone would believe you," Clara explained. "That's not a risk that any good leader would be willing to take though, and so, they would have you killed. Dragon shifters always have to put their own kind first."

"You would kill me," Darryl confirmed, his voice barely above a whisper.

It didn't matter if his statement was a question or not. Clara didn't know what to say, but if the situation arose, she knew what the alliance would demand of her. She wouldn't have a say in the matter. It was an upsetting and uncomfortable reality, but a reality nonetheless.

Chapter Ten

A piercing scream resonated through the air. It was quickly succeeded by the sound of shattering glass.

"That came from downstairs!" Clara exclaimed.

Alarmed, she swiftly turned to face Darryl, her ears picking up the panicked footsteps echoing in the corridor.

As scales began to form on her arms, she spoke firmly.

"Don't leave this room under any circumstance," she demanded. "Barricade the door. Stay clear of the window. Apart from me and Lucian, you mustn't let anyone in. Do you understand?"

Darryl remained silent, his eyes widening as another scream reverberated from within the corridor. Clara rushed forward and assertively cupped his chin, urging him to focus. He blinked sluggishly, appearing dazed.

"This is serious! Do you understand what I need you to do?"

"Yeah," he replied, evidently still disorientated.

As Clara released Darryl's chin, her hands started morphing into claws. Exiting the bedroom in haste, she slammed the door shut behind her.

Upon reaching the ground floor, she discovered shattered glass and bloodstains on every surface, coupled with the presence of several corpses. With no time to think, she flung herself in front of Sarah's daughter, Gemini, shielding her from a snarling enemy dragon.

The predator sank its sharp teeth into Clara's arm, shredding her clothes in the process. As she transformed, she was able to wrench her arm away. She maintained her position between the child and the enemy shifter, growling and baring her teeth as the rabid dragon attempted to advance.

As she used the strength of her tail to keep Gemini at a safe distance from the aggressor,

Clara speculated that this was all related to the recent crimes in the area.

Lucian and Sarah were nowhere to be seen, but out of the corner of her eye, Clara spotted numerous other dragons streaming in through the broken windows. Some of them were smaller than her, their spines adorned with sharp metal daggers. Others had wings large enough to cloak and strangle even the most resilient of victims to death.

Clara's heart throbbed with growing intensity as the dragon she had first encountered sprang forth. After a struggle, with her claws extended, she clamped down on the creature's leg. Shocking it with a jolt of electricity summoned from within, she was able to flip it over onto its back.

Something heavy crashed down at Clara's side, knocking her off balance and creating a gap between her and Gemini. Growling, she scrambled back to her feet, her tail whipping back and forth as she scanned the two dragons heading towards her.

"She's with me," shouted an assertive voice.

Clara turned her head to observe that Darryl

had gathered Gemini up in his arms and was holding her tightly. As she stood motionless in fright, a set of jagged teeth clamped down on the hinge of Clara's left wing, right near her shoulder blade.

She let out a piercing shriek, and then flailed her claws aimlessly. Sensing resistance from another enemy dragon, within seconds, she had them pinned beneath her.

Her top priority was to shield Gemini and Darryl from harm. After emitting a menacing roar, Clara mercilessly electrocuted the enemy with a short, sharp, violent jolt. Once the beast's body went limp, she swiftly searched for any remaining threats.

With large clawed feet thumping against the floor, an enemy dragon was pursuing Darryl up the staircase, steadily closing in on him. Frantically flapping her wings, Clara attempted to intercept it with a height advantage, but her movements were clumsy. She watched with dread as the dragon clamped its teeth around Darryl's ankle. The shocking agony was so intense that he dropped Gemini on the landing.

As three more enemies leapt in front of him,

and with Clara momentarily outnumbered, Darryl had no other option than to hobble out of the alliance headquarters. Once he was out of sight, Clara's rage consumed her. She growled and blindly clawed at anything and everything within her grasp. She saw only red as she relentlessly tried to eliminate any potential threats, desperate to make the house secure.

The only sound that could break through Clara's murderous rage was Gemini's cry. Becoming immediately airborne, she flew rapidly up over the stairs, her focus now solely on the child. She assessed Gemini quickly, finding only a minor cut on her cheek. Darryl had managed to protect her.

Clara remained standing between Gemini and any potential attackers, but no more appeared. It was her first opportunity to take stock of her condition, and she realised with a start just how much blood had coated her scales.

Despite the pain, Clara shifted back into her human form. Turning her focus towards finding Darryl, she assumed that he was still outside.

"Everyone must gather in the meeting

chamber," Lucian's voice boomed throughout the house. "Be there in ten minutes, or else. And where the hell are Gemini and Sarah?!"

"I've got Gemini over here!" Clara shouted as she picked up the child.

Lucian raced up the stairs and quickly took his daughter from Clara's arms, pulling her close to him as tears streamed down his face. They drew clean streaks down his blood and debris-stained skin. Gemini cried into her father's shoulder.

"Your help is greatly appreciated," Lucian told Clara.

"I'm not the one who deserves thanks," she replied. "It was Darryl who saved Gemini."

Lucian's expression became serious.

"Put some clothes on," he said. "We need to talk about what we're going to do next."

Clara's expression darkened. She wasn't interested in discussing the next steps. Her priority was to find Darryl and make sure that he was ok.

Upon entering her bedroom, Clara forcefully shut the door behind her and began pacing around restlessly. She feared that she hadn't seen the last of the enemy dragons, and given the size of the town, there were probably more of them hiding somewhere.

Whilst getting dressed, she gazed at the picture of Darryl that she had taped to the mirror. They had gone for a walk in the country on a day out, and he had posed for her. She knew it was cheesy and silly, but she loved to look at it anyway.

The more she stared at the photo, the more her sense of impending doom grew, as though the world she knew was on the verge of collapsing.

As she descended the stairs, Clara knew that going after the enemy dragon shifters alone was not an option. For her to have even the smallest chance against such danger, the alliance would have to be behind her. As she thought about how brave Darryl had been in saving Gemini, she was certain that Lucian would be willing to do whatever was needed to rescue him – and to eliminate the enemy.

One Of The Dragons

Chapter Eleven

The noise in the meeting chamber was greater than usual. With a collection of first aid supplies situated in the centre of the table, shifters were dressing wounds as they offered comfort to those who had suffered losses from the attack. Thankfully, not everyone had been present at the headquarters during the intrusion, otherwise the number of casualties would have been higher.

As he paced back and forth, Lucian addressed the alliance with stern authority.

"We've got to determine the origin and motive of the rogue shifters. It's obvious that they weren't simply tracing a scent. There has got to be more to it than that. Although we can't predict their next move, I won't allow the alliance to suffer again."

Clara sat down and gazed at the town map, meticulously examining each location. As she took note of every spot in which an abduction had occurred, a shiver ran down her spine, sending a cold sensation throughout her entire body.

"We must locate these rogue dragon shifters and ensure they pay for their heinous acts," Lucian declared. "Not only have they brutally murdered some of our own, but they have also abducted one. It's unforgivable. We shall track down these monsters and mercilessly tear them apart."

As the walls of the chamber reverberated with encouraging cheers, some members had queries, leading to whispers spreading from one person to the next. Despite the gravity of the situation, Clara smiled because Lucian had referred to Darryl as being one of their own. With this declaration, the rest of the alliance would be compelled to acknowledge him as such.

"It's safe to assume that we outnumber them," said Lucian. "However, what we don't know, and haven't prepared for, is their level of expertise. Our training sessions have been inadequate, and several of you have continued to skip them."

Lucian directed a meaningful look at Clara, causing her to feel uncomfortable and prompting her to awkwardly shift her gaze towards her hands.

"Let's not dwell on that though," he said hastily, eager to proceed. "Upon the conclusion of this meeting, we will commence our search for the enemy shifters. Before we move on, does anyone else have anything to contribute?"

He looked around, but nobody spoke up. Most were bidding farewell to their loved ones, getting ready to entrust their children's care to other alliance members should the worst happen.

"Alright then," he said. "You are all free to go. Clara, can I have a moment of your time, please?"

Clara frowned. She was eager to leave and commence her search for Darryl. She was desperate to rescue him. She couldn't bear the thought of him being killed – or unwillingly transformed into a shifter.

"Oh no!" Clara whispered, looking up at Lucian. "I think I know where the enemy is coming from!"

Lucian briefly glanced at her before directing his attention back to the map. His eyes widened, and he balled his fists at his side upon comprehending what Clara had said. The enemy dragon shifters were the abducted humans who had been transformed by the mastermind behind the attacks. Over the last few weeks, the rogue shifter had probably been trying to construct an army to use for their own means. Clara cursed herself for not having realised this fact sooner. There had, after all, been many dragons to fight during the assault on the headquarters.

"I should have known," she said.

"You might not be the most skilled in battle, but your intellect is an essential resource for this alliance," said Lucian, his tone a comforting one. "I must remember to appoint you to the war council once all of this has ended."

"Of course," Clara answered. "Assuming we survive this."

"Let's check out where we think the first attack took place," Lucian said. "The parents moved out to a new place shortly after their child went missing. I bet there's a shifter living there as we speak."

"What do you think their motive was for coming here?" Clara asked.

"I have no idea," Lucian replied. "But I'd put my life on the line that it's related to you somehow."

Clara felt a sense of guilt creeping over her as she listened to Lucian. She watched him pace around and nodded in agreement when he suggested they leave to search for Darryl. As they got into his truck, she silently prayed that they would get there in time. She was determined to make amends for what had happened, even if it meant spending the rest of her life trying to do so.

Chapter Twelve

After a short drive, Lucian parked the truck a safe distance away from the suspected house. Situated on the outskirts of the woods, it was spacious, with no adjacent buildings on either side. A perfectly discreet location, it was entirely plausible that the first attack had happened there.

"I have to ask," Clara said. "What makes you so certain that this has something to do with me?"

Lucian gave a casual shrug as the dim moonlight seeped through the truck window, casting a glow on the side of his face.

"Recently, it seems that everything that has been happening is linked to you in some way," he said. "I don't mean this to sound horrible, but ever since Darryl entered your life, things have been going wrong. I'm happy for you, really I am, but there's someone out there who doesn't agree."

Clara stepped out of the truck and slipped her hands into her trouser pockets.

"But who?" she asked. "Olivia made her objections clear, but she's dead now."

"Olivia wasn't the only shifter capable of holding a grudge."

As Lucian got out of the truck, Clara acknowledged that whoever was after her, their identity and motives remained unknown.

Perhaps there are several other shifters out there with a grudge against me. Or perhaps it could even be something to do with my parents!

Although it was a long time ago, Clara's parents had been in debt to a violent criminal gang. Aware that she was perhaps clutching at straws by this point – and possibly even being a little paranoid – she couldn't dismiss a single possibility.

Lucian headed towards one side of the house while Clara went in the opposite direction. The dilapidated building had been in a state of disrepair for a long time, even before the victim's parents had left. The surrounding area was still marked off with yellow police tape.

Blood stains were visible on the grass and the exterior walls of the house. Broken windows and the moan of the wind emanating from the woods added to the ominous atmosphere.

Clara carefully stepped onto the porch, trying to remain as silent as possible, but the boards still creaked and rattled under her feet.

She was grateful for her heightened senses, which enabled her to hear movement coming from inside the house. The sound was distant, indicating that whoever it was, they were underground somewhere.

Clara caught Lucian's attention with a wave and gestured towards the truck. They both quietly made their way back to it for a brief meeting.

"What is it?" Lucian asked as he kept his eyes fixed on the house. "Did you hear something?"

"I heard breathing – multiple sets of it, I think," she said, her voice low as she leaned in closer to him. "We could be walking into a trap. Maybe we should wait for backup."

Darryl's voice echoed in Clara's mind, urging her to be brave and not to give up. Deep down, she knew it wasn't the time to retreat.

"Are you alright?" Lucian asked, placing a hand on Clara's shoulder. "We won't have another opportunity to catch them off guard like this. They're under the impression that we're still recovering back at the headquarters."

Clara nodded in agreement, her jaw clenched. She took a few steps towards the house before glancing back at Lucian over her shoulder.

"Ok," she whispered. "Let's do this."

Catching up to her, Lucian nodded with noble determination.

The pair briefly paused in preparation for whatever it was that they were about to face. Lucian quickly sent a message to Sarah on his phone. With no time to lose, he put it back into his pocket just as fast. The moment had arrived, and Clara could feel the urgency of the situation; she sensed that Darryl was counting on her.

Chapter Thirteen

The inside of the house was in a chaotic state, indicating that the previous occupants had been struggling even before the attack.

As she surveyed the scene, Clara couldn't help but draw parallels to her childhood. The wallpaper was peeling and blemished with the residue of cigarette smoke, and the laminate kitchen worktop had warped in places where the offending items had been snuffed out. As she scanned the area, she spotted needles and spoons scattered around next to depleted lighters.

The cupboard doors dangled precariously on their hinges, and the carpets were stained with blood. It was evident that the attacker had shown no mercy. Highly aware of the possibility that a predator could be lurking in the shadows, Clara moved cautiously in the hope that she would be able to defend herself if necessary. The atmosphere in the house was so menacing that it was difficult to tell the difference between paranoia and genuine cause for concern.

Lucian signalled to Clara, and then indicated towards a door leading down into the basement. She nodded in agreement and motioned for him to take the lead.

With a stern expression, he cautiously opened the door, making sure not to create any noise. He proceeded to descend the stairs with great care. Clara braced herself before following him into the murky abyss.

As they made their way further down, she began to sense that the basement was unusually deep, far exceeding the typical depth of a residential property's lower level. As they continued to descend, the sound of voices resonating from below grew increasingly louder. A feeling of dread washed over Clara as it dawned on her that she and Lucian would be drastically outnumbered.

Enveloped in the inky blackness with only the sound of voices to guide her, with each step, she felt as though she was marching towards her demise. Overwhelmed with fear, she instinctively placed her hand on Lucian's shoulder, determined not to lose sight of him.

After what seemed like an eternity, they arrived at the bottom of the staircase and were greeted by a faint glow on the floor. Ahead of them was a series of alcoves. An unmistakable noise, the cacophony of snarls and laughter emanating from the alcove to their right confirmed that the enemy dragon shifters were present. In contrast, the alcove to their left was silent. Clara couldn't help but wonder if Darryl was lurking somewhere in the shadows – feeling both afraid, and hopeful of being rescued.

With her instincts guiding her, she signalled to Lucian to trail behind her.

Having searched through multiple vacant spaces, her heart sank as she realised that they were running out of places to investigate. She firmly believed that Darryl must be concealed somewhere within the basement; there was no way that his captors would want him to break free. If he had already been turned into a dragon shifter, they would have been even more reluctant to present him with an opportunity to turn against them.

Despite the dire circumstances, Clara clung to the possibility that Darryl had not been turned.

However, she knew this to be an optimistic hope, for whoever was behind this was intent on increasing their numbers. It would be futile to assume that Darryl was exempt. Even so, if he had indeed been converted, Clara found solace in the fact that he would be better equipped to defend himself.

With a deep breath, she mustered her courage and stepped into yet another dimly lit room. Despite the pervasive gloom, she could make out a faint illumination emanating from a window positioned high above their heads. And there, nestled underneath it, was Darryl, huddled atop a squalid mattress. His ankles were secured by a thick chain, which was tethered to the wall with a deep-set anchor.

"Whoever did this must have been planning it for a long time," Clara whispered to Lucian. "Something like this would have taken years to figure out and execute so flawlessly. Even expanding the basement to this extent would have taken a long time, and doing it without getting caught would have required a lot of effort. It all makes sense now; the rogue shifter must have turned many people to make this possible over such a short period of time."

As they moved closer to Darryl, Lucian spoke

in an even quieter whisper.

"If we're fast, we can get Darryl out of here without anyone noticing."

Clara gently moved Darryl's hair away from his face. He looked exhausted as he struggled to focus his gaze. Not only was his usually-immaculate clothing dishevelled, but his arms were scratched and his breathing seemed laboured too.

Clara felt a surge of anger coursing through her as she fully acknowledged the extent of Darryl's condition. She vowed to track down the aggressor responsible for this and exact vengeance for the harm they had caused.

Lucian interrupted Clara's thoughts by placing a hand on her shoulder. She gave a nod of recognition and leaned in closer to examine Darryl's ankles. The wound from the dragon's bite was infected and oozing with pus and blood. Trying to keep calm, Clara checked it for shifter venom.

Relieved that there was none present, she sighed heavily. As she began to work on the chain, it dawned on her that because Darryl was still fully human, she and Lucian would have to defend him should they encounter any enemy dragon shifters on the way out.

As scales started to cluster together on her arms, Clara watched her nails extend and transform into lethal claws. She glanced over her shoulder and then inserted a single claw into the lock near Darryl's ankles. After twisting it around for a moment, she finally heard the satisfying sound of a click. The lock opened, and the chain dropped away.

"What are you doing?" Darryl whispered.

"We're getting you out of here," Clara replied.

He started to chuckle softly. He seemed to be in a delirious state from the shock of what he had endured.

"Don't worry," he groaned. "My head is killing me. Can we just go home?"

Clara touched the back of her hand to Darryl's forehead. It didn't feel as though he had a fever, but judging by the state of where he had been bitten, the possibility of infection was high.

"How are you feeling?" she asked.

"It wasn't a pleasant experience," he remarked with a hint of amusement.

"We can catch up later," Lucian said firmly. "Right now, our priority is to get out of here."

A voice spoke up from behind them.

"I can't let you do that."

One Of The Dragons

Chapter Fourteen

Clara was filled with complete astonishment as she glared at the woman standing in the doorway.

It can't be!

"Mother?!" she exclaimed with shock and disbelief. "I thought you were dead!"

With a derisive laugh, the woman began to advance towards Clara, causing her to position herself in front of Darryl. Recognising that Clara bore a deep grudge against her mother and was prepared to retaliate if provoked – especially in defence of Darryl – Lucian placed himself between the woman and Clara.

With a grin, the woman bared her sharp teeth.

"You can't speak to your mother like that," she slyly taunted. "I would have expected you to have better manners after all this time, but it appears that you haven't."

Clara was certain that she could feel the beginnings of a full shift coming on. As the excruciating pain burned through her insides, she believed that she deserved it. In her mind, she was responsible for the pain and grief that everyone else was experiencing. The weight of her guilt was immense, and was compounded by the realisation that she had caused countless innocent humans to be taken away from their families, condemned to a life of violence.

Nevertheless, she was determined to put a stop to her mother's attacks on the innocent.

"You're not my mother," she declared with a vicious snarl. "You're nothing but a drug addict who happened to give birth to a child."

Having overheard the confrontation, many enemy dragons were now surrounding their leader. Positioning themselves behind her in a show of defence, they were prepared to protect her at all costs.

As the woman drew near, Clara and Lucian stepped back, taking care to keep Darryl protected. Clara was resolute in her commitment to defend Darryl, even if it meant fighting to the death to provide him with the opportunity to escape. He hadn't asked for any of this, and she was damned if he was going to lose his life to it.

Lucian cleared his throat and proceeded to speak softly to the woman in a hushed tone.

"We're willing to hear you out," he said. "Let's talk about this. What do you want?"

He was mistaken to believe that adopting a conciliatory demeanour would prove effective in dealing with Clara's mother. Clara had always known her to be stubborn and vicious.

Perhaps it's just as well that I ran away that night. Now that I've seen her like this, I don't owe her anything.

"When we were ambushed by a dragon shifter many years ago, your father perished, feeble moron that he was," said the woman. "Unlike him, I survived. The dragon shifter transformed me into one of their kind, and since then, I've been much improved; more powerful than ever, and ready to fight. I managed to remain hidden for years, but upon learning that you had developed feelings for a human, I knew that I had to eliminate you. You were never particularly bright as a child, and it seems that you've remained equally stupid to this day."

Clara's reaction was immediate and intense as she let out a deafening scream and charged towards her mother, bypassing Lucian in the process. Her claws slashed at her target, and it was unclear whether the cries were coming from her mother or from Darryl. Completely consumed by her rage, it didn't matter to Clara in that moment. Blood sprayed in all directions as she found herself quickly surrounded by dragons.

Fully transformed, Clara viciously attacked her opponents. Her claws ripped through the flesh of anyone who dared to get close. Despite being greatly outnumbered, her anger and determination made her relentless. With each pounce, she aimed to kill, snarling as she electrocuted the enemies with precise jolts of lightning. Blood coated her scales as she fought on.

Determined to protect Darryl, she battled fiercely against the endless waves of dragons. Despite her efforts, more of them continued to appear, making a victorious outcome seem impossible.

As Clara backed away from the attackers, a surge of panic threatened to overwhelm her. Suddenly, she heard a loud roar and turned to see Lucian in his full dragon form, attacking one of the enemies. Grateful for the unexpected help, she caught her breath and glanced towards her mother, who was still in human form and watching the chaos with sadistic glee. Despite the woman's wounds, she didn't seem to care about the pain, treating the fight as a twisted game.

Clara couldn't help but feel a twinge of pity for the woman, who evidently valued point-scoring over and above her own survival. Accepting that she wasn't responsible for her mother's poor choices, Clara charged at her once more. The woman was quick and evaded the attack. She grabbed hold of Clara's tail and ruthlessly plundered a knife into it.

Clara hunched over as the metallic agony seared through her every nerve. As soon as the initial shock had dissipated though, with her wings spread wide to command the space, she began to circle around her mother. Despite feeling dizzy from the blood loss, Clara refused to give up. They were on the brink of freedom, and she couldn't let it slip away.

The relentless attacks were coming from all directions, but Clara was determined as she fought off the enemy dragons while Lucian protected Darryl.

She launched herself at her mother once more. Just as she was about to catch up with her, the woman abruptly turned around and fled. Even in her human form, she was agile and swift. Clara quickly took flight and pursued her up the stairs, through the house, and into the backyard.

As the cool air rushed onto her scales and gave her a newfound awareness of her wounds, Clara felt a brief moment of relief upon noticing what was happening up ahead. Led by Sarah, the alliance was emerging from the woods. They soon rushed towards the house and burst inside to assist.

"I thought I had brought you up to be better than this, Clarabellina," her mother chided. "Yet here you are, willing to murder me in cold blood. It's such a shame that it's come to this. Can't you do any better for yourself?"

Upon hearing her mother call her by her full name, Clara snapped. She let out a thunderous bellow that echoed into the woods, and then lunged at her mother. The woman cried out in pain as she fell to the ground, writhing in a desperate effort to escape. Clara, driven by intense fury, used all of her weight to hold her mother down. Then, with every fibre of her being, she summoned an intense voltage from within. She kept her eyes closed as she sent surges of violent lightning into her mother's body. The luminous sparks surrounding them continued to crackle and hiss until Clara was certain that she was holding nothing more than a corpse.

Confident that her mother would never be able to harm anyone again, Clara quickly moved away from the remains. Everything around her immediately merged into a cacophony of dull sounds and dark, muted visuals. As an overwhelming wave of nausea consumed her, everything went black.

Chapter Fifteen

Upon regaining consciousness, Clara found herself back at the alliance headquarters in her bedroom. As she surveyed her surroundings, she had no clear indication as to how long it had been since she'd passed out.

As she slowly sat up, pain coursed through her body in waves, causing her to groan in discomfort.

After knocking gently on the door, Darryl opened it slightly and popped his head through the gap.

"I'm glad you're awake," he said cautiously. "Please get some more rest though. I don't want you to rip your stitches."

"I promise to be careful," Clara replied.

"You must be. I thought I was going to lose you. I can't bear the thought of being without you,

Clara. I love you."

The sincerity in Darryl's expression told Clara everything. She was glad to have him around and wanted to share her future with him.

"I love you too," she said, blissfully happy as she fell back against her pillows.

Despite the fresh waves of pain that erupted in her ribs, she couldn't help but feel overjoyed.

As Darryl moved to settle down next to her on the bed, they lapsed into a comfortable silence, holding on to each other compassionately. Despite the multitude of questions that they both had for each other, they were content to simply be in the moment.

***

At some point during the day, Clara and Darryl had dozed off. Clara was the first to stir, and decided to let Darryl sleep. As she gingerly got out of bed, she made sure not to fall back over. A glance in the mirror revealed the extent of her injuries. Scars crisscrossed her body, the top of her shoulder was torn, and her smile had been marred by a claw. She was a different woman after everything that had happened.

It was worth it, and I'd do it again.

Silently, she left the room and carefully descended the stairs. Each step sent a jolt of pain through her body, but she had to know if everyone was alright. She still couldn't shake the feeling that the alliance had been endangered because of her.

As soon as she noticed that the house was bustling with noise and activity, Clara felt a surge of happiness. Despite her pain, she made her way through the winding corridors towards the kitchen, from where she could hear people talking in cheerful tones.

To her relief, she found the entire alliance gathered around the table, passing plates of food around. Although a few faces were absent, the situation was better than she had feared. As she gazed upon the people who had become her family, some of the burden that had been weighing her down began to lift, and she felt tears well up in her eyes.

Smiling warmly at Clara, Lucian stood up from the table to welcome her. Despite the scars he bore from the battle, he didn't seem any less cheerful.

"It's good to see you!" he said. "We were all wondering when Darryl would finally let you out of bed. He was pretty insistent that you needed to rest."

Clara chuckled as she took a seat next to Sarah, who had already begun piling food onto a plate for her.

"Darryl cares about you very deeply," Sarah commented. "Anyway, eat up. We need you in top shape before we can promote you."

"Indeed," Lucian said. "You deserve to be promoted, Clara. After everything you've done for us, it's only right that you are. You fought off numerous enemy dragon shifters, and you're the one who figured out how to get to the source of the problem. We all owe our lives to you."

Upon seeing Darryl enter the room, Clara felt hopeful that she would be forgiven for having got out of bed.

"You were supposed to be resting," he half-jokingly scolded her. "I've got my eye on you."

Laughter erupted among everyone at the table, and Clara's grin widened as Darryl sat down to join them. He seemed completely at ease, as if he belonged there.

"I'm proud to let you know that you're now the second-in-command," Lucian told Clara, his voice authoritative, but relaxed.

Clara's food caught in her throat as she stared at Lucian in disbelief. The thought of being second-in-command was daunting, and she felt unprepared for the responsibility. Her heart raced and she began to sweat, feeling the weight of the decision bearing down on her.

"Don't look so worried," Sarah said, nudging Clara playfully. "This is a great opportunity, and you won't be alone. We're all in this together. Of course, that's if you and Darryl are planning to stick with the alliance?"

Clara was still worried. The idea of integrating a human into the alliance overwhelmed her, and she doubted her ability to lead. She had always seen herself as a loner.

"I'm not leaving," Darryl whispered, placing his hand on Clara's thigh and giving it a gentle squeeze.

Clara gave a firm nod and gratefully looked

around the large table, taking in the faces of everyone in the alliance. Though they were far from perfect, and living with them could be a challenge, she knew deep down that they were her family. She felt at ease with them, and knew that Darryl did too. No longer did she feel like an outcast. The alliance had come to accept her, as well as her relationship with Darryl.

Happy and proud to acknowledge that she was one of the dragons, Clara felt confident, and excited for what the future could bring.